by Matt Christopher

THE LUCKY BASEBALL BAT
BASEBALL PALS
BASKETBALL SPARKPLUG
TWO STRIKES ON JOHNNY
LITTLE LEFTY
TOUCHDOWN FOR TOMMY
LONG STRETCH AT FIRST BASE
BREAK FOR THE BASKET
TALL MAN IN THE PIVOT

Tall Man in the Pivot

illustrated by
Foster Caddell

by
Matt
Christopher

TALL

MAN

IN THE

PIVOT

Little, Brown and Company
Boston · Toronto

Published simultaneously in Canada
by Little, Brown & Company (Canada) Limited

PRINTED IN THE UNITED STATES OF AMERICA

To my sisters, Mary and Celeste

Tall Man in the Pivot

1

CHUCK O'NEIL lifted a drawstring bag out of the pocket of his buckskin jacket. Holding it up, he shook it gently. Its contents rattled.

"Exactly twenty-five marbles in here," he declared. "How many of them would you guys like to win?"

He wasn't worried about losing any of the shining marbles in the bag. He had won most of them, anyway.

Mickey Talbot and Steve Walters, walking on either side, looked up at him.

3

"Are you crazy?" snapped Mickey, his brown eyes flashing little angry sparks. "Our game starts at five-thirty!"

"But it's not even five yet," said Chuck calmly. "We can play hits an' spans all the way to school, and get there in plenty of time."

Chuck knew he would win the argument over Mickey; he always did. And if Mickey agreed to play, Steve would, too.

"Sometimes I wonder if you like marbles better than basketball," said Mickey disgustedly.

Mickey's disgust didn't bother Chuck. Matter of fact, hardly anything seemed to bother Chuck O'Neil. He wasn't the brightest student in the seventh grade at Milton Central, yet the kids had voted

4

him president of the class. He was by far the tallest and the skinniest.

He didn't mind being the tallest, since it helped him make first team on the basketball squad. He played center. But he wished he wasn't so skinny. Kids called him "Skinny," "Beanpole," and "Stilts." He didn't like those names, but he never let on he didn't. He had found out that when he got sore they only made more fun of him.

"Come on, you guys," said Chuck. "I know you have marbles with you. I heard them in your pockets."

"Okay. You win," said Mickey. "Come on, Steve. Let's clean him this time."

"Clean him?" echoed Steve. "Him with his long fingers? Anybody's crazy to play with him!"

But both Steve and Mickey brought out six or seven marbles each. Chuck's eyes lit up at sight of the bright-colored glass marbles. Some were of different sizes, too. They would certainly be a beautiful addition to his collection. He had a gallon jar at home half filled with marbles.

"I'll lead," said Chuck, and tossed his shooter, a large lemon-colored marble, in an arch up alongside the macadam road. It struck the ground, hopped along a little way, rolled a bit, then settled in a tiny hole.

Steve shot next, purposely tossing his pale-blue shooter about ten feet ahead of Chuck's. It struck a pebble, glanced almost straight up, then came back down to earth and stayed there.

6

"Oh, nuts!" said Steve.

A pleased smile appeared on Chuck's face.

Mickey, shooting last, dropped his marble at his feet.

Chuck's turn. He picked up his shooter, looked at Mickey's, then at Steve's. Steve's, he decided, was the easier target. He aimed at the marble, and shot. His shooter looped through the air, came down, and struck Steve's squarely on the top!

"A hit. Give me two," said Chuck.

Two for hits, one for spans. Steve stuck his hand into his pocket, brought out two marbles, and handed them to Chuck.

"Thank you," said Chuck gratefully.

Then he studied Mickey's marble. Too far away, he decided. He turned and

tossed his marble carelessly ahead of him. It struck a stone, bounced back, rolled a few inches, and stopped.

Steve laughed. He aimed his shooter at the marble, and very carefully tossed it. It missed Chuck's shooter by an inch, bounced into soft dirt, and stopped.

Steve rushed forward eagerly, crouched, and spread out his right hand between the two marbles. The tips of his thumb and little finger touched the marbles, and he let out a cry of triumph.

"Oh, well," muttered Chuck. "I'm still one ahead of you."

The one became two again. And then four. Chuck won from both Mickey and Steve, until his pocket felt heavy with marbles.

"Hey!" Mickey exclaimed suddenly.

9

"We'd better hurry to school or we'll be late!"

"Don't worry," said Chuck. "There's lots of time."

"Oh, yeah?" cried Mickey. "If we're late, it's your fault, Chuck! And Coach Veers wants us there fifteen minutes before the game starts!"

Chuck looked over at the western horizon. Soon the sun would be touching the distant hill.

"Let's go!" he said.

He poured his winnings — nine of them — into his bag, pulled the drawstring, and ran after Mickey and Steve, who were already running hard toward the school.

They pulled open the big door and hurried down the almost empty corridor. From the gym came shrill cries, and

Chuck knew, even before he and his two friends looked through the doorway, that the game between the Milton Condors and the Marathon Royals was already under way.

"I told you!" Mickey cried. They ran into the gym, alongside the court, to the locker room. Not once while they were changing into their uniforms did Mickey and Steve speak to Chuck.

Chuck was last to finish dressing. He didn't mind the remarks of the few fans as he passed before them, but Coach Veers looked at him with annoyance.

"I suppose you were playing marbles, too?" he asked.

Chuck nodded. "Yes."

Coach Veers threw out his hands hopelessly. "Playing marbles, when you knew

11

we had a basketball game? Don't you or Mickey or Steve care if we have a team or not?"

Chuck looked at Mickey and Steve sitting on the bench, their faces glum.

"It was my fault we were late, Coach," confessed Chuck. "I asked them to play with me."

"Thanks for being honest about that," said Coach Veers. "But you boys are sitting out this quarter."

Chuck sat down next to Mickey. The score on the electric scoreboard read 7 — 1 in the Royals' favor.

2

CHUCK sat with his knees high in front of him. He watched the game as if he were a spectator. He couldn't get very excited about it. He'd rather play, though, because it got dull, just sitting there.

He could tell that sitting on the bench bothered Mickey. Mickey was as restless as a bird inside a cage. Anybody could tell he was itching to be out there on the court.

"Why don't you sit still?" said Chuck.

"You're not going in until the second quarter. Coach Veers said so."

All Chuck got was a dirty look.

The clock showed two minutes and forty-eight seconds to go before the end of the quarter. There was still a long wait.

Milton, in their bright green and white suits, seemed to be helpless out there on the court. They were running hard all the time, but seldom did they have the ball. It kept popping out of their hands like a hot potato.

A Marathon man sank a set shot to make it nine points for them. Then, as right guard Howie Greene passed the ball to Dodo Burns from behind the out-of-bounds line, an alert Royals player broke in fast and intercepted the pass. He laid the ball up against the boards for another two points.

"They're sinking us!" cried Mickey, pounding his fists against his knees. "Let us go in there, Coach! Please!"

Coach Veers sat with his lips pressed tightly together. He kept looking at the clock.

"The next time," he said seriously, "you'll know better than to get here late."

Mickey's chin dropped. He jabbed an elbow against Chuck's ribs.

"It's your fault!" he said.

Chuck winced from the blow, but he didn't say anything. What was there to say? He had admitted it was his fault.

Just wait till the second quarter, he thought. *If those guys in red don't rack up twenty points first!*

15

Suddenly Dodo stole the ball from a Royals man and dribbled it all the way down the court. A man raced after him. Just as Dodo leaped to shoot, the man struck his wrist.

Shre-e-e-e-k!

Foul! And the basket counted!

The Milton fans screamed lustily for Dodo. He pushed up the shot. Made it!

4 to 11.

That was the score when the quarter ended. Then both teams huddled with their coaches. Coach Veers had Chuck and Mickey report to the scorekeeper and called out the substitutes. Now the regulars were in the game: forwards Dick Hines and Mickey Talbot; guards Dodo Burns and Howie Greene; center, Chuck O'Neil.

Presently the horn blew. The second quarter was ready to start.

Chuck stood almost a head taller than the opposing center. Easily, he tapped the ball to Mickey. Mickey dribbled down-court and passed to Dodo near the left corner. Dodo started in with the ball, and nearly lost it to a fast guard. He bounce-passed to Mickey coming in quickly to-ward him. Mickey made a turn toward the basket, but he was stopped, too. Mara-thon was certainly playing a strong zone defense.

Mickey passed the ball out to Chuck. Chuck waved it over his head a couple of times, shot it to Howie, then rushed in. Howie leaped, as if to try for a basket. In-stead, he passed it back to Chuck, who was running in toward the basket. Chuck

17

took the pass, pivoted, and leaped, hooking the ball over his head. Gracefully, it arched and swished through the hoop for a basket.

Marathon took out the ball, moving it to their front court quickly. Milton's tight defense, and Chuck's height, kept them from getting too near the basket. Marathon tried a set, missed, and Chuck caught the rebound.

Carefully, Milton brought the ball back down the court. Seconds later Chuck moved his man out of position again with nice footwork, and scored another layup.

Milton slowly began to gain. Mickey was too anxious, though, and fouled a man who was ready to shoot a set. The man was given two shots, and he sank them both.

Eight to thirteen, Marathon's favor.

Mickey took the pass from out-of-bounds, and dribbled the ball down-court. He passed to Chuck. Just as Chuck started to dribble, his man stole the ball from him and dribbled it hard toward his own backcourt!

A lone Marathon man was down there, yelling for the ball. His teammate shot it to him, and the man laid it up easily.

Chuck groaned. He had practically given them that basket himself.

A little while later the quarter ended, and the teams walked to their locker rooms for the half intermission.

3

"TOO much dribbling," said Coach Veers. He was standing between the two rows of benches on which his team was sitting. "Do more passing. And keep your passes shorter between you, so there will be less chance of interception. Chuck, you're pretty tall compared to most of the other boys. Unless you move faster that little fellow guarding you will steal the ball every time. Chuck, did you hear me?"

Chuck was trying to make a little boy laugh. The little boy was Timmy Short.

He was standing near the team with his grandfather Amos Short, the white-haired janitor. Timmy wasn't more than three years old, curly-haired and blue-eyed.

"I heard you, Coach," Chuck said.

"We did very well in our first game against the Tioga Hawks," went on Coach Veers. "No reason why we can't get out there this second half and pull this game out of the fire. What do you say?"

He made a fist of his right hand and swung it in front of him in a short, swift arc.

The team responded with an ear-splitting *"Go!"*

Chuck spoke to Mickey before they went out of the locker room.

"Mickey," he said, "you're not still sore at me, are you?"

"Forget it," replied Mickey.

"We can't win if you're going to stay sore at me," insisted Chuck. "I promise I won't ever make you late again."

"A lot of good that will do us now," answered Mickey, and ran out of the locker room before Chuck could say anything more.

That Mickey, thought Chuck. He takes everything seriously. You'd think I had made us late on purpose.

The second half got under way. The Condors took the tap and with short, quick passes had the ball on their side of the court. Forward Dick Hines sank one from the corner, then Dodo stole a pass from a Marathon guard, whipped the ball to Chuck. Chuck raced down for what he figured would be another easy layup.

24

But just as he started up with the ball, a shoulder hit his arm. The ball was knocked out of his hands. It rolled out-of bounds and struck the wall.

"Two shots!" shouted the referee.

Chuck made the first shot. The second rolled around the rim. Rolled again, then went in!

The score on the Condors' side continued to mount slowly, while that on the Royals' side hardly moved. Then the Royals rallied, and once again pushed quickly ahead of the Condors.

In the fourth quarter the Condors tied the Royals — 22 to 22 — and both teams struggled hard to forge ahead. Then the Royals called time.

After time-in was called, Chuck found himself guarded not by one man, nor two men — but three! It hardly seemed fair.

Come on, you guys. They have me crowded. It's up to you!

Then Mickey fouled!

"Oh, Mick!" groaned Chuck.

Mickey's face colored.

The players lined along the free-throw line. Chuck, crouched between two Royals players, waited for the foul shot with pounding heart.

Silence as the referee gave the ball to the Marathon player. Silence as the player took it, wiped his brow, bounced the ball a couple of times, and then measured the basket with his eyes.

Swish! A perfect throw!

That put the Royals ahead, 23 to 22. And the clock on the wall said one minute and forty seconds!

26

Howie tossed in the ball from out-of-bounds to Chuck. Chuck passed to Mickey. They moved it cautiously down-court and across the center line toward their basket. Three Royals players were surrounding Chuck again. He hardly had a chance.

Suddenly a Royals man stole the ball from Dodo! Like fleas leaving a dog, Chuck's guards tore loose from him. But Chuck was faster than he seemed. He broke after the man with the ball. Just as the man was going to throw a pass, Chuck reached out. His hand slapped the man's elbow. Everybody in the big room heard it.

Shre-e-e-e-k! went the referee's whistle.

Chuck's heart sank as far as it could sink.

There! I've done it now!

Once again they lined up along the Royals' free-throw lane. Once again silence fell. Across the short distance to the seats, near the doorway leading to the basement, stood white-haired Amos Short. With his small, birdlike eyes, he was watching, too.

The ball arched beautifully as the Marathon player threw it, aiming it first with both hands, then following through with only his right.

Swish!

24 to 22.

Fifty-five seconds to go!

The Condors took out the ball and passed it carefully but quickly down the court. Howie to Mickey, Mickey to Chuck, and then to Dick and Dodo. Like fleas returning, the guards were back on Chuck. But now they had more difficulty keeping near him. It was as if he had wound up his legs.

Then he saw his chance. Breaking toward the basket, he shouted for the ball.

Mickey heaved it, keeping it high. Chuck caught it on the tips of his fingers. In the same motion he tossed it toward the basket. As he did so, a Marathon man pushed him.

The ball dropped through the nylon net as the whistle shrilled. But the basket counted.

The fans screamed as Chuck stepped leisurely to the free-throw line and waited for the referee to give him the ball.

The score was now 24 to 24.

And the clock said only fourteen seconds to play.

The screaming died away, and Chuck was handed the ball.

"One shot," said the referee.

One shot. That was all. He had to make it, or the game might have to go into an overtime period.

He bounced the ball, felt it big and light in his hands. Then he looked at the basket, took aim, and tossed the ball in a high, graceful arch.

It dropped, pierced the netting with hardly a whisper, and fourteen seconds later the game was over.

Condors won, 25 to 24.

In the locker room, Chuck received praise for his remarkable shooting. But Coach Veers was a stern man. Win or lose, the boys had to abide by the rules.

"All of you made a beautiful comeback in that second half," he told his players. "But this is a warning: Anybody late or absent without a good reason will be indefinitely suspended from playing."

He means Mickey and Steve and me, thought Chuck. *Especially me.*

"Don't forget practice tomorrow at two o'clock," reminded the coach. "Now get showered and go home."

Chuck showered and dressed. He felt in his jacket pocket for the broadcloth bag.

The bag was gone!

Chuck searched his locker. The lockers were built in two rows, one on top of the other. Chuck's locker was the very last one, on the bottom.

The bag wasn't in the locker. Chuck searched the floor.

There it was, sticking out underneath the locker. It was partly open. The drawstring was loose. Chuck dumped out the marbles and quickly counted them.

There were six missing!

4

CHUCK got up early Saturday morning. He looked out of the living room window and saw the sun splashing the street with gold. What a beautiful day! Mr. Horn, the mail carrier, was delivering letters to the Wallaces, and Dave, the bread man, was carrying his basket of baked goods to the Burnses.

Down the street two girls were playing hopscotch. A short, stout boy in a blue jacket was teasing them. It was Steve Walters. He was trying to play hopscotch

33

along with the girls, and they didn't like it.

They finally chased him off.

Steve came up the street, whistling as he walked. There was no tune to his whistling. He just whistled.

He saw Chuck standing in front of the window, and waved at him.

"Hey! Want to play hits an' spans?" he yelled to Chuck.

Hits an' spans? Well, why not? Six marbles were missing from his bag. They had to be replaced.

"I'll be right out!" Chuck yelled back.

His mother hurried into the room to find out what he was shouting about. He explained that he had just yelled to tell Steve Walters he'd be right out.

"All right, but I don't want you to be gone all day," she warned him. "It's a good

34

day to mow the lawn. We won't have very many nice days like this left before winter hits us."

"Don't worry, Ma. I'll mow it," promised Chuck. "I just want to win at least six marbles first!"

Chuck looked closely at the marbles Steve took out of his pocket. Some of them were very much like his but he couldn't be sure that any of them had come from his marble bag.

Anyway, Steve wouldn't have taken them.

Chuck had won three marbles from Steve by the time Mickey Talbot and Terry Malley came along and joined them.

"Hi, pivot man," greeted Mickey, smiling.

Chuck grinned. "Hi, Mick. Hi, Terry."

35

How good he felt all of a sudden! Mickey wasn't sore at him any more. Mickey was his best pal, and Chuck would rather lose a hundred marbles than lose Mickey's friendship.

"Let's just play hits. No spans," suggested Steve.

Chuck glowered at him. "Nothing doing. Hits *and* spans."

"Then I'm out," said Steve, pocketing his shooter.

Chuck looked at the others. Apparently neither Mickey nor Terry cared whether it was with or without spans. But Chuck knew he had the advantage at spanning. His fingers fanned out at least two inches more than any of the other three boys' fingers did. So, it really wasn't fair playing hits *and* spans with them.

36

"Okay," agreed Chuck. "Just hits."

They played on the O'Neils' hard-packed, cindered driveway. Chuck's lemon marble looked like a tiny sun as he tossed it in an arch some six feet ahead of him. It struck the hard surface, bounced, then rolled to a stop.

Mickey aimed at it, but missed it by two inches. His shooter rolled on and finally settled.

Steve, anxious to win back some of his marbles from Chuck, aimed carefully at the lemon marble. His pale blue shooter hardly arched as it headed directly at Chuck's shooter.

Click! A hit!

Steve smiled from ear to ear, and held out his hand toward Chuck.

"That's two, please," he said.

Chuck handed over two marbles. When his turn came again, three shiny marbles, all of different colors, glowed in various places on the driveway. Two times three is six. With careful aim, and a little stretching, he just might be able to do it.

Mickey's marble was the nearest. Chuck rolled the lemon shooter around in his hand, then braced it gently between his thumb and first two fingers. Taking careful aim, he tossed the shooter. Like a satellite the lemon marble arched, winking in the sun, and dropped right on top of Mickey's shooter!

Now for Terry's. Terry's shooter was bright crimson with white streaks through it, a very pretty marble. Again taking careful aim, Chuck shot.

Click! Another hit!

"Pretty lucky," said Steve. "But you have to be awful good to hit mine."

Steve was right. His blue shooter was about five feet away, lodged against the jutting sidewalk. An inch or so this side of it grew a weed, a leaf of which practically hid the marble from Chuck's view.

Even stretching on this one won't help, thought Chuck. *I'd better not even try.*

"Go ahead," Steve dared him. "Afraid you'll miss and I'll get you? What's two marbles?"

Chuck looked at the fat boy, and then at the marble. Saying nothing, he rubbed the lemon marble again between the palms of his hands, then held it between his thumb and first two fingers.

He shot, and groaned. Even as the marble left his fingers, he knew that he had thrown it too far to the left.

But a strange thing happened. The marble struck the weed on the side, glanced off, and hit Steve's blue shooter squarely on the top!

Mickey and Terry roared. Chuck, pretending it was nothing, held out his palm toward Steve.

"What's two marbles?" he echoed. "Two marbles, that's all."

Steve didn't say a word.

By the time they finished playing, Chuck had won fourteen marbles, more than enough to replace those that had been taken from his marble bag.

He mowed the lawn, then in the afternoon went to the school gym. He took his bag of marbles along, just in case some-

body wanted to play after basketball practice.

Milton's Condors were already in the locker room, getting dressed for practice. Steve was pulling his white jersey over his barrel-like chest as Chuck walked in.

"One side, everybody! Make room for the marble champion!" cried Steve.

Chuck lifted the bag out of his jacket pocket. It bulged with forty marbles.

"Anybody who'd like to try to win some of these can see me after practice," Chuck joked.

He returned the bag to his pocket and walked down the aisle to his locker. Mr. Amos Short was sitting on the end of the bench, one scrawny knee draped over the other.

42

"Hi, Mr. Short," greeted Chuck. "Where's Timmy today?"

"Left him home," said Mr. Short. "Too tough to handle at times. Say, you played a nice game of ball the other day."

"Thank you, Mr. Short."

"Ever hear of Neal Thompson?" asked Mr. Short. "Well, no, you wouldn't. That was long before your time. He played with the Stars, you know. Was a center, just like you, and he had an eye like a hawk. I remember once —"

There he goes, thought Chuck, telling about old-time basketball days again. He was still talking when Chuck finished dressing.

Coach Veers had the boys work on passes and jump shots. Then they shot from the free-throw line. Chuck watched Steve Walters miss nearly every shot he tried. The coach instructed him on how to improve his throwing, but the more Steve tried the worse he got. Finally, tired and perspiring, he left the court.

He must've gotten so disgusted he went home, thought Chuck.

When practice was over, the team, exhausted and sweaty, headed for the locker room.

Chuck showered and dressed. As he walked away from the locker room, he felt for the marble bag in his pocket.

It was still there. It hadn't been touched.

5

CHUCK didn't miss any marbles the next week, either. But he began to wonder if it was Steve Walters who had taken those six.

Maybe Steve was unhappy because he couldn't play basketball very well. Maybe he was unhappy because he couldn't win marbles from Chuck.

On Tuesday the Condors traveled to Sherman and played the Wasps. They had heard that the Wasps had a fast, classy team, and already had trounced

45

the St. John's Ravens 42 to 19, and the Tioga Hawks 47 to 22.

The Condors could almost smell defeat as they stepped on the court.

"Look how tall those guys are," wailed Dodo Burns. "No wonder they've been trouncing everybody!"

"Not everybody," said little Mickey Talbot. "They've only played two games."

The Wasps began showing their stingers early in the first quarter. They sank three baskets for six points. Then Mickey's guard bumped into the little forward as he dribbled down-court.

A foul was called. And Mickey, shooting with extreme care, made the shot.

6 – 1.

The Wasps took the ball from out-of-bounds and practically flew with it down

46

across the center line toward the basket. But Chuck got in front of a pass, pulled it down, and dribbled all the way back up the court for another two points.

Both teams scored a few more baskets each before the quarter ended. Coach Veers, kneeling in the huddle among all his players, smiled with satisfaction.

"That's a nice brand of ball you're playing out there," he said encouragingly. "Just keep it up. Chuck, it's up to you to get those rebounds. You're the only tall boy we have!"

The Wasps had one boy taller than Chuck. He was their center, a blond boy with freckles sprinkled all over his shoulders. Time after time he and Chuck went up for the rebound and came down with the ball clutched tightly between them.

47

Before the second quarter ended Mark Jackson went in for Dodo, and Mel Weston for Howie. Chuck wondered if Coach Veers would put in Steve. But he didn't.

The score was locked, 18 — 18, at the half. The Condors, relaxing in the locker room, could not have been happier if the game was over and they had won it.

"We'll take them," said Chuck, bright-faced. "Just watch and see."

In the third quarter the Condors crawled ahead of the Wasps.

"We must've clipped off their stinger!" shouted Chuck to Mickey, as they ran down-court after sinking another basket.

"Don't count your chickens too early!" advised Mickey.

The Wasps dumped another, but that was evened up, too, when Mickey shot a quick pass to Chuck and Chuck leaped and arched one that banked against the boards and through the hoop.

The big electric scoreboard on the wall clicked off the seconds rapidly. Just below it the score stood out in glaring red figures. Already it was in the middle twenties, seesawing first in favor of the Wasps, and then the Condors.

Then Dodo sank a set shot from the corner.

Now they were one point ahead of the Wasps.

The Wasps worked the ball swiftly to their end of the court, and lost it when Mickey darted in like a dragonfly and snatched the ball from the hands of a Wasps player. Like a machine, the Condors passed the ball back up the court.

Chuck, standing in the keyhole, waited for a quick pass to sink one before time ran out.

Shr-e-e-e-k! The whistle!

"Three seconds!" shouted the referee.

Chuck stamped his feet angrily. He had forgotten that on the offensive he shouldn't have stood in the free-throw area that long. It was a violation.

The Wasps took the ball out-of-bounds.

It was nip and tuck again in the fourth. Then the tall Wasps center, unable to pass to any of his men, tried a long set — *and made it!*

That put them ahead 38 to 36.

Half a minute before the game was over Mickey committed a foul, and the Wasps player sank the shot.

39 to 36.

The Wasps won.

"Well, at least they didn't swamp us," said Mickey, as they filed into the locker room. "Maybe we can beat them the next time."

Chuck sat down tiredly. He had played all but two or three minutes of the game.

He found himself sitting beside Steve Walters, who hadn't worked up a single bead of sweat.

"We nearly took that one," said Chuck.

"I don't care if we did or didn't," replied Steve unhappily. "I'm just a bench warmer."

Chuck felt sorry for the fat, husky boy. Steve had been in the game for a minute, but had hardly touched the ball.

I know I should feel sorry for him,

51

thought Chuck. But I don't. I think he took the marbles out of my bag.

During practice the next week, Chuck kept his marbles home.

On Thursday the Condors had a home game with the Dalton City Darts, and struggled hard to win by a close score, 37 to 33.

6

THERE was practice, as usual, on Saturday afternoon at 2 o'clock. It had rained during the morning, leaving a dampness in the air and puddles in the driveways and on the streets.

Things like that didn't discourage Chuck from playing marbles. But his usual victims — Steve, Mickey, and Howie — did not want to play. Nevertheless, he carried the marble bag with exactly twenty-five marbles in it to school with him.

Coach Veers drilled the team on short

passes and foul shots. Many times foul shots, the coach informed them, determined the win or loss of a game. Every player should become good at them.

Then Coach Veers paired off two teams and had them scrimmage. He put Mickey and Chuck on the same team so that they could work together developing their pass plays. These plays usually ended with Mickey's passing the ball to Chuck and Chuck's sinking the basket.

Steve Walters was on Chuck's side, playing guard. After a while Coach Veers took Steve and another boy out, and put in the two boys still sitting on the bench.

Steve sat down, wiping his perspiring body with a towel. Presently he rose, walked around the court, and out the door leading to the locker room.

Where is he going? Chuck wondered.

Steve had not handled the ball very much in the scrimmage game. He was slow, and whenever he shot at the basket his throw was seldom near the hoop. That was why the other players hardly ever threw the ball to him.

He's sore, Chuck figured. *He's going home because he's sore.*

And maybe he'll want to take some more of my marbles now that he has a chance!

"Coach!" cried Chuck. "Could somebody go in my place for a second? I'll be right back!"

Coach Veers looked at him, then waved in a boy from the bench. Chuck sprinted for the locker room.

He found Steve opening a locker a cou-

ple of doors away from his. Slamming it shut, he turned and stared at Chuck.

"Hi, Chuck," said Steve, his eyes widening in surprise. "What are you doing here?"

"Me? What are *you* doing here? That wasn't your locker you just closed."

"I made a mistake," said Steve, his face coloring. "Mine is this next one. Why? What are you so excited about?"

"I think you took my marbles," Chuck said.

"Me?"

"Yes, you! And you were going to take some more just now. Only I caught you in time before you found the right locker."

Steve's round face grew red as a tomato. He opened his locker, took out his clothes, and began to dress quickly.

"I don't know anything about your marbles, except that you're always winning from me. That's all I know," said Steve. "Don't you say I took them. I get mad because I'm a lousy player. I can't run and I can't shoot baskets. I can't do anything. I don't know why I still like to play, but I do! But don't you say I took your marbles! I never took anybody's marbles in my life!"

7

THE CONDORS played the St. John's Ravens at St. John's Junior High School. The walls of the old gym were cracked, and in several places plaster had fallen off, showing the bare laths underneath. Streaks scarred the floor. Instead of bleachers, a single line of benches was strung around the basketball court.

"They're building a new school next year," Coach Veers said to the boys as they walked from the gym to the locker room. "Looks as if they need one."

"Maybe that's why they have a losing team," said Chuck. "They haven't won a game yet."

As the boys changed into their green and white suits, Chuck noticed Steve tucking in his jersey. This was Tuesday. Steve hadn't come around at all since practice last Saturday.

Since the Ravens were not so hot, maybe Coach Veers would let Steve see more action today. As he sat on the bench thinking about Steve, Chuck was pretty well mixed up. He thought Steve had taken his marbles, yet Steve had acted awfully honest and sincere when he denied it.

I just don't know what to think, Chuck said to himself.

Coach Veers used the regular starting line-up: Dick Hines and Mickey Talbot in the forward slots, Dodo Burns and Howie Greene in the guard positions, and Chuck jumping center.

Chuck's man was three inches shorter than he. Chuck, filled with all the confidence in the world, stood relaxed in the center circle. This little towhead facing him might as well sit this game out. He wouldn't have a chance.

The referee blew his whistle, and up went the ball.

Up went the Ravens center, too, higher than Chuck! And tapped the ball to a Ravens guard!

Chuck's eyes popped.

"Come on, Chuck! Let's go!" yelled Mickey.

Before he was able to go, however, the Ravens had the ball far down on their end of the court. A curly-haired boy snared a short pass under the basket, went up, and laid the ball against the boards. Down it went through the hoop for two points.

So the Ravens scored first. Who said they were a poor team?

Mickey was yelling again, trying to coax some life into the overconfident Condors.

Fast and eager, the Ravens stole the ball from Dick and once again tore down the court. A series of short passes, then another layup.

Four points!

"Let's wake up!" cried Mickey.

It was Mickey himself who put the Condors back into the ball game. Really, Mickey and Chuck. They worked their pass play toward the basket. Then Chuck, receiving a short pass from Mickey, leaped, turned, and very easily tossed the big orange ball through the net.

Dodo fouled a Ravens player, resulting in another point for the Ravens. Chuck sank another, and as the seconds ticked quickly by, both the Condors and the Ravens sank an almost equal share of baskets.

In the second quarter Dodo popped in two long sets, then stole the ball from a Ravens guard and dribbled all the way down the length of the court for another basket. Dodo was playing wonderful ball, doing even better with his shots than Chuck.

Dick was off. His shots missed. Twice his passes were caught by the Ravens. He was really more of a hindrance to the team than a help.

Before the quarter was half over, Coach Veers sent Steve in and benched Dick.

Some improvement that is! thought Chuck.

There were times when Chuck could have passed the ball to Steve, but he didn't. Steve would be waiting eagerly in the open. Then Chuck would pass to someone else. Steve's round face showed he was hurt.

Mickey must have felt different about Steve than Chuck did. Once when Chuck was not free to pass to, Mickey bounce-passed to Steve. And Steve, before his guard could swoop down on him, shot for the basket. And made it!

Lucky, Chuck said to himself.

But before the half ended, Steve sank

another. The score read 19 to 18, in the Condors' favor. A very slim margin.

Chuck began to feel uncomfortable. Maybe the score would have looked better if he had not been so selfish. He should have passed to Steve when he had a chance to.

8

THE second half started with Dick back in the line-up. He played carefully now, passing off to one of his teammates instead of shooting for a basket, even when he could have tried a layup.

After a minute of play Chuck dumped in a set shot from the corner. Anxious to make up the two points, the Ravens drove wildly down the court. Mickey Talbot tried to take the ball away from the dribbler, but struck the boy's hand.

Foul. One shot.

66

The try failed. Chuck and the Ravens' center went up for the rebound. Chuck's long fingers grasped the ball, brought it down, and Chuck dribbled it up-court.

He fired a pass to Dodo. Dodo bounce-passed to Mickey, and Mickey dribbled toward the basket.

His guard swung in front of him. Mickey turned, placing himself between the guard and the ball. He kept dribbling, while he looked for someone to pass to.

Chuck raced in from just outside the three-second lane. Quickly Mickey passed the ball to him, throwing it in front of the tall center. The pass was timed perfectly. Chuck caught it, leaped, and tossed the ball against the boards. It bounced back into the net for two points.

Taking the ball from out-of-bounds, the

Ravens raced wildly again with it down the court, and they almost threw it away with a poorly timed pass. The ball glanced off Mickey's fingers and bounced into the hands of a Ravens player who just happened to be in the right spot at the right time.

The player raced in for a layup and charged into Dick Hines, who fell backward against the floor. The ball riffled through the net.

"Foul!" yelled the referee, after giving a blast on his whistle. "Number Five! Basket doesn't count!"

The big hand on the time clock paused while the teams walked up-court, and Dick took his place at the free-throw line.

The referee was holding up one finger.

The players lined up along the free-throw lane, and the referee handed the ball to Dick. The dark-haired forward was nervous.

Dick bounced the ball a couple of times, then looked up at the basket and shot.

In!

"Good boy!" cried Chuck.

For a moment the Ravens had the ball again. But a player was called on traveling, and the ball went back to the Condors. A pass to Dodo, then to Howie, to Mickey, and finally to Chuck, who dropped in another through the ring.

The horn blew eerily as the Ravens asked for time out.

"I can use some rest, too!" Chuck laughed, running to the sidelines with his teammates.

"Boys, you're doing all right," smiled

Coach Veers. "Dodo, you and Howie sit it out for a while. Steve, go in for Dodo. Mark, in for Howie. Just play heads-up ball. Cover your man, and you'll be all right."

It was the Ravens' ball. They took it out, and now passed it carefully to their end of the court. Obviously their coach had cautioned them about being too reckless with the ball.

Their passwork was an improvement. But when they tried to shoot a basket, the ball struck the ring, bounced off, and Chuck caught the rebound.

He passed to Mickey, and Mickey dribbled across the center line. With three seconds to go, he tried a set, and made it.

The third quarter ended.

9

THE RAVENS started the last quarter with a lot of spirit. They passed the ball swiftly between them, advancing it quickly toward their basket. But they had little chance to shoot. The Condors' defense was like a wall.

Then the Ravens' center, catching a swift short pass from one of his men, made a fast break for the basket. He drove between Mickey and Chuck with no caution. Just as he started up with the ball, Chuck's hand snaked out. He wanted to lay his hand on the ball and stop the player from trying the shot. Instead, he hit the boy's wrist. The referee's whistle pierced the air.

"Two shots!" said the official, lifting both hands and spreading his fingers to indicate Chuck's number.

The Ravens center sank the first shot. The second struck the side of the ring, rolled around it, and fell off. Ball in play, men from both teams rushed in for the rebound.

Chuck's long fingers pulled it down, but a boy in blue and white yanked it from him. As if it were covered with grease, the ball squirted from his hands and in and out of other anxious, grasping fingers.

A mad scramble followed, ending with Mickey and a Ravens player both lying

73

on the floor, their arms wrapped around the ball as if it were alive.

Jump ball!

Mickey tapped it to Dick. Dick flipped it to Chuck, and Chuck to Mark. Once across the center line, the Condors found that the Ravens seemed to have multiplied in number. There seemed to be eight instead of five of them, they pressed the Condors so hard.

Once a Ravens player knocked the ball from Chuck's hand, but Chuck quickly retrieved it. From backcourt, he bounce-passed to Mickey cutting across in front of him. Then he raced in, crossing the free-throw lane toward the corner.

Mickey handed the ball to Steve. Steve dribbled, almost losing the ball to a

Ravens player as the opponent swept in from behind him. But Steve pulled the ball out of the other's reach, pivoted, and passed to Chuck. Chuck went in and laid it against the boards.

The ball wobbled through the net for another two points.

In spite of the Ravens' hustle, they could not halt the Condors' mighty drive. At the final buzzer, the score was Condors 49, Ravens 28.

Returning home on the bus, Chuck and Mickey sat together. Ahead of them sat Steve and Mark Jackson. The two boys were chatting happily about the game. Chuck knew it was because they were thrilled at having played more in this game than they ever had before.

"Heard you boys smeared the St. John's team yesterday."

Amos Short's beady eyes twinkled as he stepped into the locker room. With him was Timmy, eyes like large moons as he looked at the players towering before him.

"Sure did, Mr. Short," replied Howie. "Forty-nine to twenty-eight."

"Who are you playing next?"

"The Spencer Badgers. Next week."

"They'll be a cinch, too," said Chuck.

"Don't be so sure," said Steve, his eyes meeting Chuck's directly. "You're always so sure."

His voice lacked friendliness, and Chuck looked at him hard.

"I'm sure about a lot of things," said Chuck. There was a touch of anger in his voice. Amos Short looked puzzled, and Chuck turned away with embarrassment. He hung his buckskin jacket inside his locker, then took off his shirt.

Coach Veers put the Condors through a grinding pace. When time came for the practice session to end, the boys' bodies glistened with sweat. They were glad to feel the cooling spray of the showers.

Mickey and Chuck walked from school together, and talked about the coming game with the Badgers. As they crossed the street they heard the cries of two little boys playing on the lawn behind the white picket fence of Daniel Short's place. One was Timmy. The other was Davey Smith, Timmy's neighbor.

Right now the small boys did not ap-

pear to be on very friendly terms. They
were quarreling about something.

"I bet Timmy started that fight," said
Mickey. "He's the daringest little kid I
ever saw."

Mrs. Short appeared at the door. She
called to the boys, and they stopped quarreling immediately.

Chuck and Mickey waved to her. She
waved back, then covered her bare arms
with her apron, gave a final warning to
the boys, and disappeared into the
house.

"Bet in a little while they'll be battling
again!" laughed Mickey.

They soon separated. Not until Chuck
reached home and removed his jacket did
he think about counting the marbles inside his marble bag.

This time there were seven missing!

Chuck still wanted to blame Steve. He couldn't remember seeing Steve leave the court during their practice, but he could have done so. *After all, I can't watch him every minute, can I?*

Anyway, who else could it be? Who else, if it wasn't Steve?

Chuck thought hard about it. Sometimes he was sure it was Steve who had taken his marbles, but most of the time he wasn't really sure. *How can I make sure?*

Saturday afternoon, he saw Steve walking all by himself on Burke Street. Burke Street was a dead-end street. Beyond it lay a small woods, and beyond the woods a high bank of earth piled up like a wall. On the other side of that wall was a stone quarry, from which limestone was trucked to all parts of the country.

Chuck followed Steve through the woods. The trees were mostly birch and spread far apart. The leaves had fallen, making a soft brown carpet on the ground, and there was an autumn smell in the air.

If Steve turned around, he would easily see Chuck. But he didn't turn around in the woods. When he was climbing the high bank he turned and saw Chuck. "Chuck! What are you doing?"

"I want to see you," said Chuck. "Wednesday, seven more marbles were missing from my bag!"

"You crazy nut!" shouted Steve. "I didn't take them!"

Then he scrambled to the peak of the bank and vanished over the other side.

Chuck hurried after him. Running off like that proved Steve was guilty, he thought.

Chuck started a small landslide as he ran up the bank after Steve. He reached the top, looked over, and saw Steve at the bottom.

Steve wasn't moving. Both of his feet were sinking in mud which was already up to his ankles. He couldn't get out.

He looked up at Chuck, and for a while Chuck just looked down at him.

Steve was like a trapped rabbit.

10

I can't move!" Steve cried helplessly. "I'm stuck!"

Chuck couldn't leave Steve stuck in the mud. No matter if Steve had taken his marbles, he had to help him.

Chuck started down the side of the bank.

"Be careful!" cautioned Steve. "I got going fast and couldn't stop! That's how I landed in here!"

Chuck went slowly and stopped at the foot of the bank.

He stepped as close to the mud as he dared. He even stepped a little into it, but the toe of his shoe sank in and he drew back. Steve was at least six feet away.

"Don't walk in here or you'll get stuck, too," said Steve.

"The only thing I can do is run back for help," said Chuck. "I'll see if the Pierces are home."

Steve's face was pale. "Please hurry, Chuck, I'm still sinking!"

Chuck scampered up the bank and down the other side. Then he ran as hard as his legs could go.

It's my fault, he told himself. *It's my fault Steve is stuck in that mud. He would not have rushed down that bank so fast if I hadn't upset him.*

Mr. Pierce and his seventeen-year-old

son Johnny were in the garage, working on their car.

Breathlessly, Chuck told them what had happened to Steve and please-get-something-to-help-Steve-out-because-the-mud-was-deep-and-he-was-far-out-in-it.

"Hold on! Hold on!" Mr. Pierce said, picking up an orange cloth and wiping his grimed hands on it. "Let's start all over again. Where did you say Steve is?"

This time Chuck explained Steve's predicament a little slower, and Mr. Pierce understood.

"Come on, Johnny," he said to his son. "I'll put on my fishing boots, and we'll see what we can do about rescuing this boy's friend." Johnny, a tall, broad-shouldered boy, was a front court man on the varsity basketball squad.

It didn't take Mr. Pierce long to pull on his boots. In hardly any time at all Chuck was leading the way through the woods to the bank. When they reached the top and peered over Steve looked somewhat different to Chuck. Steve's hands and sleeves were covered with mud. So were the backs of his pants and jacket.

"I got help!" Chuck shouted down to him. "Don't worry! We'll have you out in a minute!"

"I tried to move again and I fell," confessed Steve. He looked ready to cry.

The Pierces descended the bank cautiously.

"Did you forget your mud shoes?" Mr. Pierce asked, smiling.

A grin erased the panicky expression from Steve's face.

"I guess so, Mr. Pierce! Think you can get me out of here?"

"I'm sure of it," said Mr. Pierce. "Johnny and I have pulled more people out of mud than you'd care to count."

Steve laughed.

Slowly, Mr. Pierce walked out into the mud toward Steve. The mud seeped up to his ankles, and he had difficulty picking up his feet. But at last he reached Steve.

He took the orange cloth out of his jacket pocket, wiped the mud from Steve's hands, and told Steve to put his hands behind his neck. Then Mr. Pierce lifted Steve's right foot out of the mud, placed it on his knee, and lifted out Steve's other foot. Then he put Steve behind him, so that Steve was riding him piggy-back.

Slowly Mr. Pierce came trudging out of the mud. He set Steve down on solid ground, and began wiping the mud off himself with the orange cloth, which was pretty muddy itself by now.

"Thanks, Mr. Pierce," said Steve. "I guess I'll catch it when I get home."

"One thing you should catch when you're home," advised Mr. Pierce, "is a bath. What made you walk in that mud? Couldn't you see it?"

Chuck felt his heart begin to pound.

Tell Mr. Pierce it was my fault. Tell him I was chasing you because I blamed you for taking my marbles! Go on! Tell him!

"I didn't see it in time, I guess," said Steve. "I just ran down the bank and there it was. Before I knew it I was stuck in it!"

"It's a good thing that both of you didn't

89

get into it together," smiled Johnny. "Then you really would have been in a mess!"

They started up the bank, the two boys leading the way.

As the Pierces headed for home, both boys thanked them again. Then Steve said, "Thanks, Chuck, for going after the Pierces."

"Thank you, too, Steve, for not telling them I was chasing you. I wouldn't have blamed you if you had."

For a while Steve was silent. Then he said, "I wish you'd trust me, Chuck. I mean it when I say I didn't take your marbles. Won't you believe me?"

"Yes, I will, Steve," replied Chuck. "I believe you."

11

LATER on that afternoon, Chuck thought of a plan to catch whoever was taking his marbles.

He showed his dad five marbles and asked him if he'd make a hole in each.

"A hole?" His dad stared puzzledly. "What do you want holes in those marbles for?"

"To catch a thief," answered Chuck. "Somebody's been taking my marbles right out of my marble bag, and I don't know who is doing it. I might find out if I had holes drilled in some of them."

"H'm-mm," murmured Mr. O'Neil, rubbing his chin. "A little detective work, I see. Okay. Let's go down in the workshop and see what we can do."

Mr. O'Neil put a marble between the jaws of a vise which was secured to the edge of his workbench. With a file he flattened a small area on the marble. Then he fitted a small drill into his electric hand drill and bored a shallow hole into the round, shiny ball.

He released the marble from the vise and showed it to Chuck. "There. How's that?" he asked.

"Great!" said Chuck.

Mr. O'Neil drilled holes into the other

four marbles, and Chuck went up the stairs, whistling merrily.

He kept the marked marbles in a small box in his bureau. No sense carrying them around with him over the week end, when he might be playing hits or hits an' spans.

He put them in his marble bag Monday, but nothing was missing from his bag after Monday's practice.

The Condors played the Spencer Badgers Tuesday afternoon. So far the Badgers had won two and lost three. That average was neither too good nor too bad. But since the game was to be played on the Badgers' home court, Mickey and Dodo and one or two others began to worry a little.

"You guys worry over every game as if it were the most important game in the world," said Chuck. "So what if we lose? Somebody has to lose."

"It is the most important," replied Mickey seriously. "Anyway, it is to me."

"Isn't it important to you?" asked Dodo.

"Sure, it's important," Chuck said. "But not that important. I never worry over any game. I play the best I can. That's all."

Chuck did, too. He proved it again on the court as he flitted about like a big bird, taking the passes from Mickey or Dick Hines, and dropping the ball through the ring with that quick, easy motion of his.

The Badgers kept up an even pace with the Condors throughout the first quarter, then fell back by four points at the end of the half.

Steve and Mel Weston went in a little

while during the third quarter. Chuck passed to Steve when he had a chance to. He was glad to be able to show Steve that everything was all right between them again.

When Steve scored a bucket, Chuck cheered for him. Steve was playing better ball than he had ever played before.

Toward the end of the third quarter the Badgers' best ballplayer was yanked from the game. He had just committed his fourth foul. One more and he would be out altogether.

The remaining Badgers could do little without him. The Condors crept ahead. With three minutes left in the final period, the good ballplayer went back in the game for the Badgers. But the damage was done.

The Condors carried home the victory, 36 to 26.

Chuck waited until he arrived home before he counted the marbles in his bag. Counting them was practically a habit, now. But no marbles were missing.

Nothing happened during Wednesday's practice, either. Perhaps, thought Chuck, he had seen the end of it. Nobody was going to take his marbles any more.

But then, after Thursday's practice, somebody did it again.

Five marbles were missing.

And two of them had holes!

12

NEXT morning a marshmallow blanket of snow covered the street and sidewalks, and lay on the branches of the trees. Flakes still tumbled silently down, and disappeared in the blanket.

"Hooray!" cried Chuck. "Hey, Mom! Did you see the snow?"

"Yes. I saw it," she said. "It had to come sometime."

During the morning, while Chuck was in school, the snow stopped. Gradually the gray sky cleared, and by noon the sun pierced through the clouds and began melting the snow.

Chuck was disappointed. He had wanted to go sled-riding after school, for there was no basketball practice on Fridays. Well, it would snow again.

Probably he could get someone to play marbles with him. Terry? Mel? Dodo? Could one of them have been taking his marbles?

Chuck didn't think so. None of them would do a thing like that. They would ask him for marbles if they needed any. Or they would buy a bagful in a dime store for a quarter.

But someone wasn't asking, and wasn't buying them, either. And it had to be someone on the ball team.

But who?

99

Chuck saw Dodo and Mel, but neither was able to play. They were going shopping with their parents. He met Terry and Dick on their way to the library and decided to go with them.

Only one book about basketball was available, and Terry took that. Dick picked out a science-fiction book, and Chuck an adventure. That night Chuck did nothing but read the book.

He awoke Saturday morning with the sun shooting rays through his window. What a difference from yesterday morning!

About ten o'clock he took his bag of marbles and went out in the cool fresh air. He headed for Mickey's house. Maybe he would see some of the gang on the way.

Basketball practice was at two, and he wanted to play marbles a little beforehand.

Presently Mickey came down the street, his hands stuck into the pockets of his jacket.

"Hi, Mick!" Chuck greeted. "You're just the guy I'm looking for!"

Mickey grinned. "Two guesses why," he said. "And the first one doesn't count. Marbles!"

"Right," said Chuck. "Got any with you?"

"Some," replied Mickey.

"Just hits?" asked Chuck.

"Hits and spans," said Mickey. "I'm no coward."

Chuck laughed. He took his big yellow

shooter out of his marble bag and tossed it about ten feet ahead of him alongside the cement walk.

Mickey held out a palmful, picked out his large black and white shooter, and put the others back into his pocket. Taking careful aim, he shot at Chuck's marble.

The marble missed Chuck's by inches, bounced a little, then stopped. Mickey leaped forward, crouched and fanned out both of his hands between the two marbles.

"Sorry," murmured Chuck. "Not quite."

Mickey groaned. Chuck picked up his shooter, hit Mickey's with it, then stood up, smiling.

"Two marbles, please. Still want to play spans?"

"Yes, I do," said Mickey, lifting two

102

marbles out of his pocket and giving them to Chuck. "I said I'm no coward. Now I'll shoot first."

He tossed his shooter.

Chuck was about to pocket the two marbles he'd just won from Mickey when one of them caught his attention. It looked very familiar.

He turned it around slowly between his thumb and forefinger, and then stared at it with wide, unbelieving eyes.

In the marble was a hole!

13

TEARS were in Chuck's eyes as he looked at the boy who had been his best friend all these years.

"Oh, Mick," he groaned. "It's been you!"

Anger swelled inside him, and he threw the marble as far as he could down the street.

Then he whirled and ran home.

"Chuck!" Mickey yelled after him. "Hey, Chuck! Come back here!"

"Keep away from me!" Chuck cried

over his shoulder. "Don't come near me!"

He didn't stop running until he reached home. He stumbled into the kitchen, breathing hard.

His mother was at the kitchen sink, changing the water in a vase. A cluster of flowers lay on the counter near her elbow.

"Who's chasing you?" she asked.

"Nobody," said Chuck. He took off his jacket, hung it in the closet, and went to his bedroom.

He couldn't believe it. He just couldn't believe that it was Mickey Talbot who'd been taking his marbles. Mickey Talbot. His best friend.

Can't a person trust his best friend? Who can you trust if you can't trust your best friend?

They had played and done everything together. Just everything. And in basketball, wasn't it their combination that helped the Condors win ball games?

What would happen to their games now? He couldn't play with Mickey. Not any more.

And their practice session this afternoon. How could he go to it and practice alongside Mickey, knowing that Mickey was the one who had been guilty all the time of taking his marbles?

Chuck felt guilty, too. Guilty and ashamed at the way he had treated Steve Walters.

Later, he ate dinner with his mother and dad. They noticed that something bothered him, but he wouldn't tell.

Then his dad said, "Did someone take

107

one of the marbles I had drilled a hole in for you? Did you find out who it was?"

Chuck didn't move a muscle for a moment. Then he nodded.

His father went on eating. He didn't ask Chuck who it was. And Chuck didn't tell him.

14

CHUCK sat in the living room, reading the adventure book he had borrowed from the library.

"Aren't you going to basketball practice today?" his dad asked. "It's twenty minutes of two."

Chuck lowered his book. He'd been thinking about practice while he'd been reading. He hated to go, though he knew he should.

He looked up at his dad. His face flushed as he met those understanding

gray eyes. His dad knew what was bother-
ing him all right. You couldn't fool his
dad.

"What do you think, son?" asked his
dad. "Don't you want to go?"

"No, I don't, Dad," said Chuck truth-
fully. "But I'd better, I guess. I'd hate to
get booted off the team, just because of"
— his lower lip quivered — "of some kid!"

His dad smiled and patted him lightly
on the shoulder. "That's the spirit, boy,"
he said.

Coach Veers split the Condors into two
teams, and had them scrimmage. However, he kept Chuck and Mickey on the
same side.

Chuck played as if nothing had happened between him and Mickey. No one

could tell the difference, except that not once did Chuck speak to Mickey. Not once did he say as much as "Mick! Throw it here!" Matter of fact, Chuck hardly spoke at all to anyone.

During a few moments of rest, Dodo asked him, "What's the matter, Chuck? Sick?"

"Sick?" Chuck forced a smile. "What are you talking about? I'm fine. Do I look sick?"

"No. But I haven't heard you say a word."

Chuck shrugged. "I don't always have to talk, do I?"

He avoided Mickey's eyes. Strange how he could feel them on him.

We're finished, you and I, Mickey.

You're not my friend any more. Friends are guys you can trust. And I can't trust you.

He felt terribly lonely. Regardless of the many boys around him, he felt a lonesomeness he had never felt before.

Mickey had been his pal. Even a brother couldn't have been closer to him than Mickey had been. Now, after what Mickey had done to him, with whom could he pal that he could trust?

Steve Walters? Steve was a good kid. He was sure of that, now. He'd been a fool accusing Steve of taking his marbles.

But Mickey had been a good kid, too. And look what he had done! *How can you tell anyone else wouldn't do it too? You just can't.*

No. He'd better not look for any more

112

pals. He'd be friends with Steve, Dodo, Howie, and the others. But not pals. There was a difference.

In the locker room, after practice, Mickey stopped beside him.

"Chuck, what's the matter with you? What have I done?"

"Go away," whispered Chuck. "Go away from me!"

"Tell me!" Mickey pleaded.

"Please!" said Chuck.

He dressed quickly and hurried home.

Tuesday afternoon, he hated to get on the bus that took the team to Windsor. But this was the last game of the first half. The Condors had won five so far, and lost one. They were tied with the Sherman Wasps for first place. If the Condors beat the Windsor Orioles, and the Wasps lost to the Darts, the Condors would be in first place. Up till today, the Orioles had won 4 and lost 2. They were no pushovers.

The Orioles center was the same height as Chuck. But he was not a beanpole. His legs and arms bulged with muscles.

Chuck outjumped him the first time and tapped the ball to Dick. Dick dribbled toward the out-of-bounds line, stopped, and pivoted. A second later he lost the ball to a quick Orioles guard.

The guard heaved the pass to his center, and the tall boy dribbled down the court with no one near him. He banked the ball against the boards for an easy two points.

"C'mon, Chuck!" yelled Mickey. "Watch him!"

Listen to him, thought Chuck. Telling *me* what to do!

The Orioles soon sank another. It wasn't hard to see that they were outplaying the Condors. Mickey dumped in a set shot from the corner, and then Dodo lifted the ball from a mad scramble and clumsily hurled it in a high arch in the direction of the basket.

The ball whistled through the net, and nobody was more surprised than Dodo.

The Orioles led as the teams went into the second quarter. Chuck realized that Dodo, Howie, and Dick were looking toward him most of the time, as if waiting for him to start things rolling.

Why me? Why should they always depend on me?

With two minutes to go before the half

ended, Mickey called time. Coach Veers huddled with the boys.

"Chuck, you're not with us," he said. "You haven't handled that ball more than four or five times this quarter. Get that ball from Mick and sink it! And keep close to your man. You can stop him. Just try it and see."

Chuck caught Mickey's glance as the team broke out of the huddle. *If I'm not with us, why doesn't the coach put in Terry? I wouldn't care a bit.*

Condors' ball. They took it out, and quickly had it zipping back and forth in a series of passes in their backcourt.

Then Chuck rushed in, took a pass from Mickey, and tried a hook. The ball rolled around the rim and fell off. Chuck and the Orioles center leaped for the rebound.

116

Chuck got it, tried for the basket, and failed again.

Now the Orioles center caught it, swiftly passed it to a forward. Chuck sighed hopelessly. He didn't even try running after the player. The Orioles made the basket, and a moment later the half ended.

The teams retreated to the locker rooms. Chuck sat in silence on one end of the bench, his elbows on his knees.

He hardly noticed Mickey sitting down beside him, until Mickey said, "Chuck, you're mad at me because of that marble, aren't you? That marble I gave you with a hole in it."

Chuck looked around at him. "Go away, Mickey. Sit somewhere else. There's lots of places to sit besides next to me."

15

MICKEY didn't go away.

"It is that marble, isn't it?" he said. "That marble with a hole in it?"

"Yes, it's that marble," said Chuck. "That gave you away. I used to think it was Steve who'd been taking my marbles. Then I found out it wasn't. I asked my Dad to drill a hole in some of my marbles for me. I thought that if anybody took one of them I'd find out who it was. And I did find out. Only, I — I never dreamed it was you!"

118

Mickey's eyes were wide. "But it *wasn't* me, Chuck! I didn't take your marbles! Honest!"

Chuck stared, bewildered. Mickey sounded very sincere.

"But you must have! You gave it to me!"

"I gave it to you, but I didn't take it. I didn't steal it, Chuck. I found it!"

"Found it?" Chuck swallowed. "Where?"

"In front of Dan Short's house. Just outside the fence."

Chuck's mind raced back. In front of Dan Short's house? Who —

Timmy! Of course! Didn't he often come with his grandfather Amos Short to the Condors' practices? And didn't he run around and misbehave so that Mr. Short had to speak to him several times?

"Mickey, it was Timmy!" exclaimed Chuck. "It must have been! Remember not long ago you and I were walking by their yard and Timmy and Davey Smith were quarreling? Mrs. Short came out and stopped them. Remember? They could have been quarreling about a marble. Maybe several of them. They could have been marbles Timmy was taking out of my marble bag!"

A big grin splashed across Mickey's face. "I bet they were, Chuck!"

Yes, it must have been Timmy. Chuck's locker was one of the lower ones, right at the end. While watching Chuck undress, Timmy could have noticed the marble bag. And when his grandfather wasn't looking, Timmy could have gone to the locker and taken out the marbles.

Boy! If Mr. Amos Short ever suspected his little grandson of taking a player's marbles, the old janitor certainly would have spanked his hide, and probably he would never bring him to the practices again!

Chuck began to smile.

"I hardly feel bad at all about it, now, Mickey," he confessed. "I guess I'm just real glad it wasn't you, or Steve, or somebody else on the team who was doing it."

Mickey got up and put an armlock around Chuck's neck. "Me too, Stilts! Now, how about you playing some real ball this second half so we can win this game?"

Chuck grinned. He clamped his arms around Mickey's waist and stood up, lifting Mickey right off the floor.

"Of course I will! But the rest of you guys must help me!"

The Condors began clicking almost the instant the starting whistle of the second half blew.

Chuck wasn't caught off guard as the referee tossed up the ball. He outjumped the Orioles' husky center, tapping the ball to Mickey, and Mickey passed to Dick in one continuous motion.

Presently the ball went back to Mickey. Mickey faked a guard, heaved a high pass to Chuck, who came running in fast, and Chuck shot for the basket.

In!

Orioles' out. But the ball wasn't long in their possession. They must have thought a hurricane hit them as Chuck leaped up from nowhere, intercepted a pass, and got the ball moving in the opposite direction.

A moment later Dick Hines sank one from the corner.

The Orioles tried hard to slow down the Condors, but the Condors just would not slow down. With Chuck and Mickey playing their best since the season had started, the Condors rolled and kept rolling.

Coach Veers put in substitutes in the last quarter. This helped the Orioles in sinking a few baskets, which were far from enough to do any good.

The game ended with the Condors winning 43 to 32.

"Well, see you fellows won the first half," grinned Mr. Amos Short at the Condors' Wednesday afternoon practice. "But don't get it in your heads that you should take it easy this second half."

"Don't worry about us, Mr. Short," said Chuck. "We'll keep playing harder than ever. Just watch and —"

He paused as he lifted his jacket out of the locker. One side of it felt real heavy. He put it on and stuck his hand into his right side pocket.

He blinked, and pulled out a plastic bag filled with marbles! Fifty of them, according to the label on the front of it!

He turned, and looked directly into the bright, smiling eyes of Mr. Amos Short.

"Compliments of Timmy Short," said Mr. Short. "We both promise he'll never take anything again that doesn't belong to him. That little mischief maker! I never knew —"

Chuck laughed. "That's all right, Mr. Short. He's real little. He could make a mistake easy."

He handed the plastic bag to the janitor. "Here, Mr. Short. Give it to Timmy. I really don't need it. I have plenty of marbles."

Mr. Short looked at Chuck hesitatingly. "You sure you don't want them?"

"I'm sure, Mr. Short."

"Okay, Chuck. I'll tell him you gave these to him. He'll like that."

Chuck swallowed. Boy, that lump had come up fast.

"Come on, Chuck," said Mickey. "Let's go."

They walked out together — Chuck, Mickey, and Steve. It was a cold Decem-

ber day. Far in the western horizon the red sun was sinking fast.

Mistakes, thought Chuck. I made some, too. I almost lost two good pals because I wouldn't trust them.

"What are you mumbling about?" said Mickey.

"Yeah," said Steve. "Speak up so we can hear you."

"Who, me?" said Chuck, blushing. "I didn't say a word!"